THE VIOLENT EARTH

FLOOD

JULIA WATERLOW

Thomson Learning
New York

september 1994

Books in the series

Earthquake
Flood
Storm
Volcano

First published in the
United States in 1993 by
Thomson Learning
115 Fifth Avenue
New York, NY 10003

First published in 1992 by
Wayland (Publishers) Ltd

Cataloging-in-Publication Data applied for

ISBN: 1-56847-003-7

Printed in Italy

Picture: A village in the Sudan partly under water after the flood disaster of 1988.

CONTENTS

FLOODS HIT CHINA

Wall of water

Sitting on a dike with nothing but water all around, the Chinese farmers said they had lost everything. They told of walls of swirling water 10 feet high tearing across their paddy fields. For a month they had slaved to strengthen the dikes against rising waters caused by heavy rainfall. On July 11, 1991 there had been yet another terrible downpour of rain.

As they stopped their work a torrent of water burst through a dike. It demolished houses and destroyed crops and machinery. "We were running for our lives," said Li Dedei, the village chief. "Huge logs that we used to support the dike were thrown into the air by water, and rocks and other debris came crashing down."

Chinese people wade through floodwater in Wuxi, a city near the Yangtze River. The summer of 1991 brought terrible floods to many parts of China.

Major Chinese floods this century

Year	River	Deaths
1931	Yellow River	3,700,000
1938	Yellow River	1,000,000
1954	Yangtze River	30,000
1991	Yangtze River	1,700

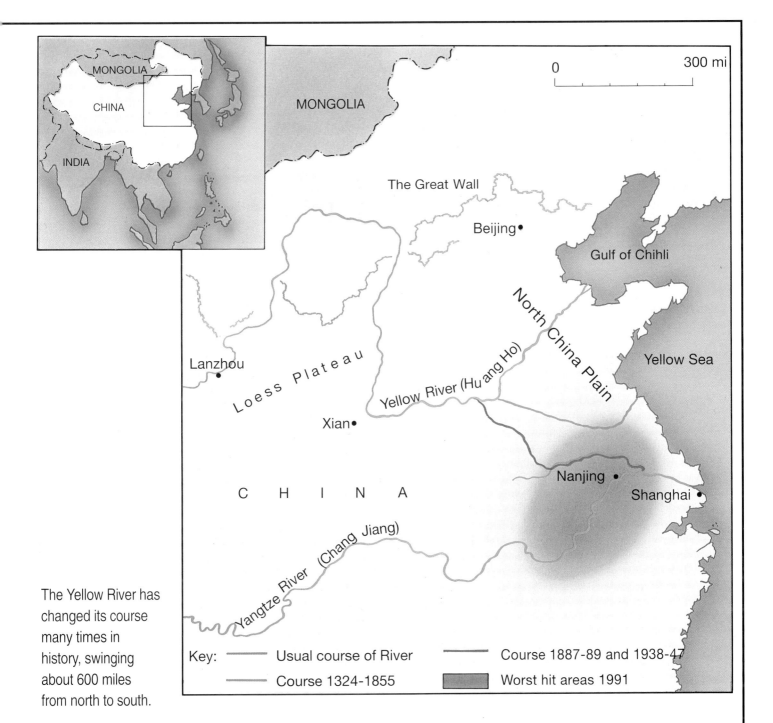

MONGOLIA

CHINA

INDIA

0   300 mi

MONGOLIA

The Great Wall

Beijing •

Gulf of Chihli

North China Plain

Yellow Sea

Lanzhou •

Loess Plateau

Yellow River (Huang Ho)

Xian •

C H I N A

Nanjing •

Shanghai •

Yangtze River (Chang Jiang)

Key: —— Usual course of River   —— Course 1887-89 and 1938-47
      —— Course 1324-1855   ▓▓ Worst hit areas 1991

The Yellow River has changed its course many times in history, swinging about 600 miles from north to south.

Crops ruined

Months of rain in China in 1991 caused floods that submerged an area of farmland larger than the state of Minnesota. People poled boats and wooden washtubs around their fields and huddled on rooftops crowded with furniture, bicycles, and livestock. The worst-hit area was the Yangtze River basin.

"We couldn't save our paddy fields...the water has washed away years of effort," said one farmer. No flooding as devastating as this had hit China since 1954 when at least 10 million people were evacuated. In 1991 more than 200 million people were affected by the floods in some way.

Disease spreads

Despite the widespread damage, fewer than 2,000 people died. But afterward, polluted drinking water caused serious illnesses among millions of stranded flood victims. The army, which was helping to rescue people, said that in badly hit areas up to 25 percent of the population was suffering from dysentery.

China's history of disaster

China has a history of terrible floods. Although there have been more than 1,000 bad floods in 2,000 years in the Yangtze River valley, the most disastrous have been caused by the great Yellow River in the north. Because of these floods the river is nicknamed "China's sorrow." In 1887 nearly 2 million people died, in 1931 the death toll was over 3 million, and in 1938 it was almost 1 million. Every time one of China's major rivers floods, millions of people are affected because so many live on the flood plains where the best farming land lies.

Controlling the floods

The Yellow River brings millions of tons of yellow-brown muddy silt downstream from the

Concrete channels divert water when floods threaten on this tributary of the Yangtze River. Flood control was first started here in the third century B.C.

hills where it rises. As it reaches the plain, the river slows and drops its sediment, not only on the riverbed but also along each bank. Natural banks, called levees, build up beside the river.

For over 3,000 years China has tried to control the Yellow River by building higher levees, dredging, digging channels, and building dams. Work done in the last 50 years appears temporarily to have stopped serious flooding from the Yellow River.

However, the river is like a sleeping dragon and may yet overflow its banks to cause terrible devastation.

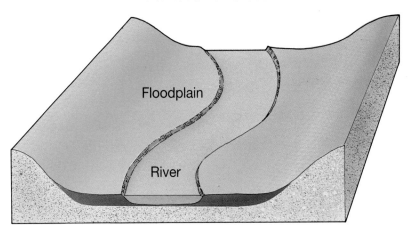

1. Water on the floodplain moves slowly, and sediment is dropped along each bank of the river.

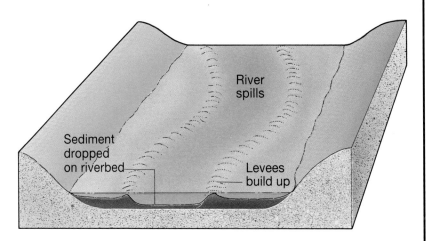

2. After many floods, sand and silt have built up ridges of material called levees.

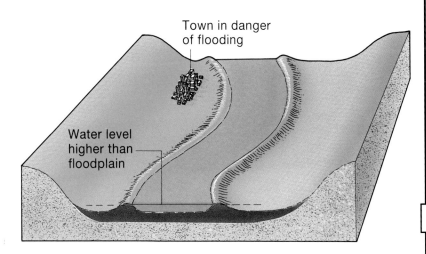

3. Slowly the bed of the river is raised and the river is contained only by the levees.

HOW FLOODS START

What is a flood?

A flood occurs when water pours over land that is usually dry. Not all floods are harmful, and if people are prepared they can control them. But most floods cause damage because they happen unexpectedly.

Rain and snow

Heavy rain can cause floods. If a lot of rain falls quickly, the earth is unable to soak it all up, and water builds up on the surface. When it runs off into rivers, the rivers sometimes overflow their banks.

This diagram shows some of the conditions that can cause flooding.

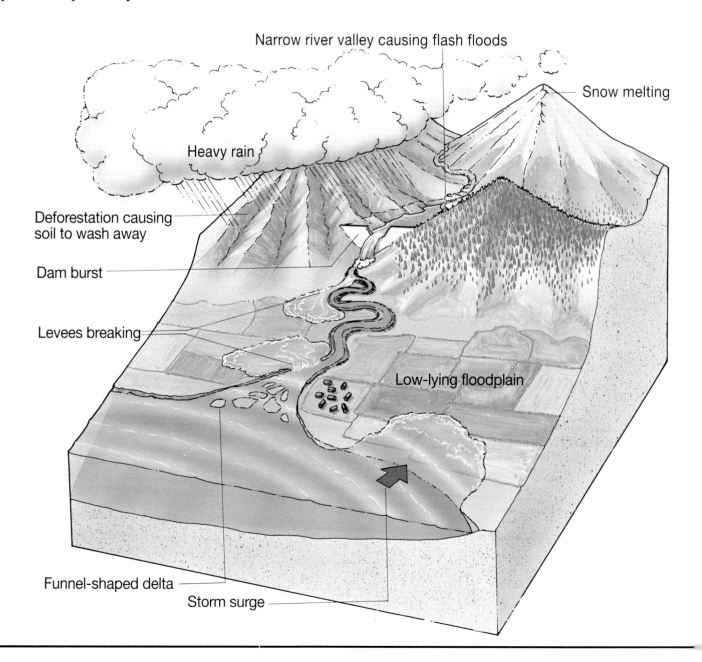

Narrow river valley causing flash floods

Snow melting

Heavy rain

Deforestation causing soil to wash away

Dam burst

Levees breaking

Low-lying floodplain

Funnel-shaped delta

Storm surge

If the river valley is narrow, the water rises quickly, reaching a level many times higher than normal. It rushes down the valley in a raging torrent called a flash flood.

In the spring millions of tons of water are released when snow melts. If there is a sudden warm spell, the snow melts very quickly. The ground and rivers cannot cope with so much water, and floods result.

Flooding by the sea

Storms at sea can create enormous waves called storm surges. If strong winds blow the waves toward the land, the coasts are flooded. This happens particularly where land is low-lying, as it is in many river deltas and along river estuaries. The effects are worse where the coast is shaped like a funnel, which directs the waves toward the land.

Terrible floods have also been caused by earthquakes and volcanoes under the sea. These sometimes cause waves, called tsunamis, which travel unseen through the ocean. When a tsunami reaches shallow water it rears up and crashes onto the land.

Waves caused by storms can rear up to great heights and pour over the land. The worst floods happen where the land is flat and low-lying.

9

FLOOD DAMAGE

The water's force

The force of rushing water as it first bursts from a river or crashes in from the sea is like that of a wall of concrete moving at high speed. Water is heavy–a large bathtub full weighs 1,500 pounds. Imagine a flood tearing along at 80 miles per hour, as one did in Florence, Italy in 1966.

Death and destruction

Mud, earth, and boulders–sometimes bigger than cars–are carried along by floodwaters. They rip up anything not firmly anchored to the ground.

In the United States in 1955, a flood washed away a wooden, four-story hotel.

When water rushes through an area, it damages everything in its path. Cars, animals, and people are picked up and tossed around like matchsticks. People die from being battered or drowned. Homes and possessions are ruined not only by the water's violence but also by substances like oil and sewage, which get mixed up in the flood. Mud gets into everything, often clogging roads and blocking drains and water pipes.

In 1988 a sudden flash flood in France picked up these cars, swept them along, and dumped them in crumpled heaps.

Floodwater pours along a street knocking over a telephone booth and running into buildings.

The problems continue

When the water settles or drains away, people often have no shelter. Roads, bridges, and railroads are washed away, and telephone lines are cut. In China in 1887, over one million people starved to death after a flood because their crops had been ruined and there was no other food. Disease spreads quickly because the floodwater is polluted and there is no fresh drinking water.

GREAT FLOOD DISASTERS

Noah's Flood

The legends of many peoples tell of a great flood thousands of years ago. The Bible tells the story of Noah, who built a boat to save animals from a flood where "all the high mountains under the whole Heaven were covered." In Iraq, between the rivers Tigris and Euphrates, evidence has been found of a massive flood about 5,000 years ago. It covered an area of about 30,000 square miles and drowned all the river valleys where people lived. Although it is still a mystery, many people believe this was Noah's Flood.

The Mississippi River

"Noah ought to have stuck around; he'd have seen a real flood," said a girl in 1927, as the Mississippi River poured out over thousands of square miles of land. There was little to see except water. Only the tops of tall trees, church steeples, and the roofs and chimneys of houses poked out above the endless mass of water that covered the land.

Heavy rain had fallen all winter and by spring the Mississippi was full to the top of its banks. It broke through its levees in 120 places.

Water from the Mississippi River surges across the countryside as a levee collapses. These floods in 1927 were called the United States greatest peacetime disaster.

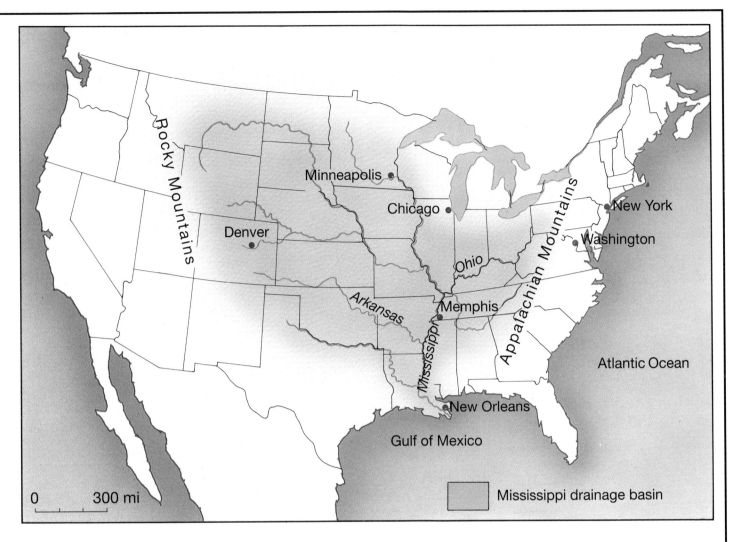

Labels on map: Rocky Mountains, Minneapolis, Chicago, Denver, Ohio, Arkansas, Mississippi, Memphis, Appalachian Mountains, New York, Washington, New Orleans, Atlantic Ocean, Gulf of Mexico

0   300 mi

Mississippi drainage basin

Mississippi River Basin Floods

1927 Mississippi:
300 deaths, 637,000 homeless, massive areas flooded.

1951 Kansas and Missouri:
41 deaths, 200,000 homeless.

1973 Mississippi:
Area larger than France flooded.

Above: The great Mississippi River draws water from a huge area. Heavy rain in one part can send a flood into other areas far downstream.

"It swept everything before it. Washtubs, work benches, household furniture, chickens, and domestic animals were floating away." (Eyewitness Turner Catledge.)

One survivor said the water rushed through like a "tan-colored wall 7 feet high and with a roar as of a mighty wind."

Costly damage
More than 750,000 houses in seven states were flooded. Huge areas of farmland were covered by water for over two months. The cost of the damage was $300 million but, surprisingly, only about 300 people died. Floods in developed countries like the United States are usually costly in terms of money; in developing countries the costs are more often in lives.

13

Bangladesh, 1970

With a force about 100 times greater than that of an atom bomb, a cyclone struck Bangladesh in November 1970. A huge storm surge, with waves higher than a two-story house, poured over the land, sweeping away everything in its path. When the water went down a few days later, it was impossible to walk without treading on dead bodies. The great tide of water claimed 40,000 lives. Still more people died because of disease or starvation resulting from ruined crops. More than one million people died in all.

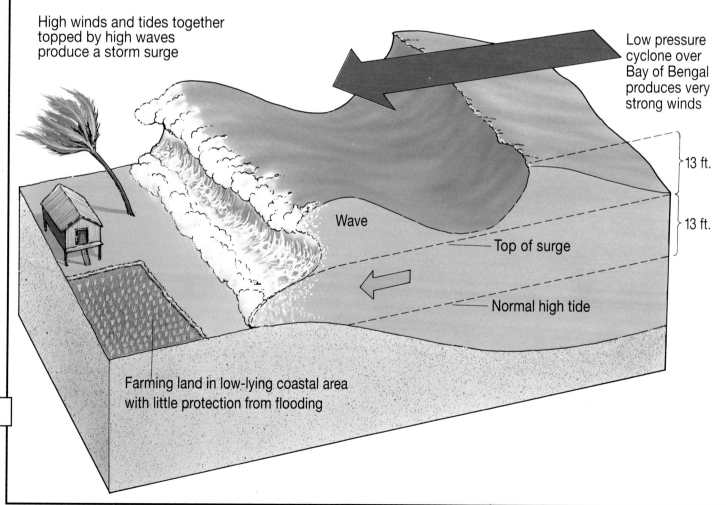

High winds and tides together topped by high waves produce a storm surge

Low pressure cyclone over Bay of Bengal produces very strong winds

13 ft.

13 ft.

Wave

Top of surge

Normal high tide

Farming land in low-lying coastal area with little protection from flooding

Left: A Bangladesh family stranded by the floods, waiting for aid to arrive.

Right: Bangladesh is hit by floods almost ever year. Houses are washed away and people have to make shelters wherever they can, avoiding the water.

"We were all sleeping when it hit at midnight. I caught hold of a palm tree and climbed it and hung on until the waters went down around dawn." (Mr. Ali Husain, survivor.)

This diagram shows the development of storm surges off the coast of Bangladesh.

Rescue

The government rescue services were slow and did not have enough equipment to launch a successful rescue operation. Because of the destruction caused by the floods, it was difficult to reach the disaster area. Money, food, drinking water, and medicines were sent from other countries to help the survivors.

Lives in danger

In Bangladesh millions of people live between the Ganges and the great Brahmaputra River and on islands in the river delta, which lies barely above sea level. Although the rivers regularly flood during the monsoon season, cyclones cause the worst devastation.

Since 1960 there have been at least 18 major cyclones causing thousands of deaths and making millions of people homeless. Very little has been done to try to control the floods in Bangladesh, and many people continue to die as a result of flooding.

Big Thompson River

On the night of July 31, 1976, campers were sheltering in their tents in a popular campground by the banks of the Big Thompson River near Loveland, Colorado. At the same time, great thunderstorms were brewing up in the Gulf of Mexico. One of these drifted northward and came to a halt over the Rockies. In four hours, 10 inches of rain–many times the normal amount for a whole month–fell on the mountains around the river valley. The Big Thompson rose from its normal depth of 1.5 feet to nearly 23 feet. Suddenly it surged down the narrow gorge, the only escape route through the mountains.

The raging torrent strikes

Everything in the river's path was crushed or washed away. Buildings were smashed into small pieces or swept whole down the valley. A power station was crushed into a pile of rubble.

This house was washed away when the Big Thompson River flooded in 1976.

"The whole mountainside is gone. There is no way. I'm trying to get out of here before I drown." (Radio message from Patrolman William Miller during Big Thompson River flood, 1976.)

Buildings in Australia damaged by heavy floods.

A survivor saw the highway ripped up, sending enormous chunks of asphalt high into the air. No one in the gorge could escape, and there had been no time to launch a rescue operation. Later, 139 bodies were found, some in cars buried 7 feet beneath the riverbed.

Australia, 1974

Some of the worst floods of this century swamped thousands of square miles of Queensland and New South Wales in Australia in January 1974. Over 10,000 homes in Brisbane were destroyed or damaged by floods after torrential rains. In the desert where rain seldom falls, 12 inches fell in 24 hours. Lakes appeared even as far inland as Alice Springs. Rivers rose to over 20 feet, and the floods killed hundreds of thousands of cattle and sheep.

Floods in Europe

Date	Place	Cause	Deaths
1952	Lynmouth, England	Flash flood	34
1953	England and the Netherlands	Storm surge	2,157
1963	Alps, Italy	Dam burst	2,000
1966	Florence, Italy	River flood	127

North Sea flood

A map showing how gale-force winds were funneled into Britain and the Netherlands in 1953.

On January 31, 1953, gales swept down the North Sea. The wild weather had already sunk several ships off Britain. As the winds pushed the sea southward, the level rose and a storm surge nearly 10 feet high rolled toward the English coast. Seawalls collapsed under the weight of the water, and floods poured into coastal towns and villages.

London under threat

The surge came up the Thames River as far as Westminster in the heart of London. It rose to the top of the wall by the Houses of Parliament and stopped just before going over it. There was nearly a major disaster. Where walls gave way downriver, 1,000 houses were flooded within minutes.

The dikes break

The Netherlands suffered far worse. "It is probable that no floods of such an intensity have occurred during the past 400 or 500 years," claimed a Dutch weather analyst. On the morning of January 31, the rising sea level seemed to stop at the top of the huge dikes built to protect the low-lying country. But they were no match for the violent storm, and suddenly the sea surged forward and broke through. Some settlements were wiped out as the water swept across them, and 12 percent of the Netherlands' farming land was flooded. About 1,850 people and over 250,000 animals were killed.

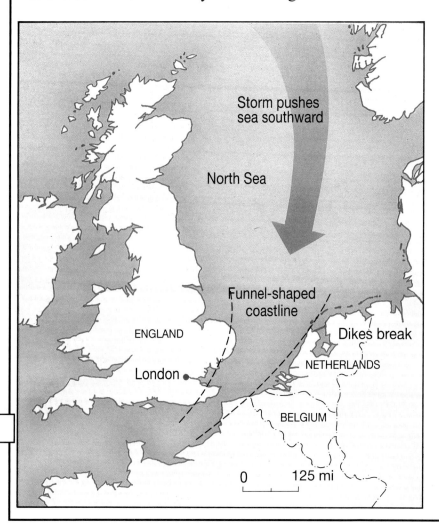

Storm pushes sea southward

North Sea

Funnel-shaped coastline

ENGLAND

Dikes break

NETHERLANDS

London

BELGIUM

0   125 mi

Right: This man has brought milk to his family, stranded in their house in Kent. In February 1953, large areas of the east coast of England were flooded after severe storms.

HELPING FLOOD VICTIMS

A helicopter rescues
families trapped by
a tidal wave that
flooded parts of the
south of France.

A survivor's story

"We sit upon the ground in groups, afraid to sleep, too miserable to cry, waiting with forlorn hope for a rescue boat. We have no water except the foul stuff that is all about us.... There is no food. There is no wood. We have no fire."

This man was stranded on a levee when the Mississippi River flooded in 1927. But the story could come from almost anywhere in the world. Telephones, roads, railroads, and bridges can be badly damaged, making it difficult for rescuers to bring help. Boats may be the only answer. Some countries use helicopters for rescuing stranded people and for dropping supplies to them.

Aid

One of the first jobs to be done after a flood is to get food and fresh water to the survivors. People may also need shelter. If the flood has destroyed crops or ruined farmland, long-term help may be needed to prevent starvation. For people in developing countries, foreign aid is very important.

Cleaning up

If the flood is too big for local services, such as firefighters, the army may be brought in to help clean up. Bulldozers and cranes are used to clear away heavy debris. Some of the worst damage to property can be caused by mud; it can take months of cleaning to remove it. Then rebuilding has to begin.

Vital food is dished out at a relief camp in Bangladesh in 1988, after floods left thousands of people without food or clean water.

21

CONTROL AND PREVENTION

People who have had to live with floods for thousands of years have come to understand what causes flooding and how they can make their homes safer. Many people have adapted their life-styles to try to prevent the devastation caused by floods.

Floodplain
River flooding occurs after a river channel has been filled, and the river spills onto the floodplain. The floodplain is a very large flat area along the course of a river or stream. A floodplain will always flood from time to time.

Houses near the Amazon River are built on high stilts. At some times of the year, so much rain falls that huge areas of land are flooded.

Right: Soil is being washed away where trees have been cut down in the Himalayas. Rain runs off the land quickly and can cause sudden floods.

Below: A forester is planting trees to replace others that were cut down. Trees hold the soil together, allowing it to soak up water instead of being washed away.

People who live on floodplains have to protect themselves. Some build their house on stilts, so they keep dry when the river floods. Others use the land only at the time of year when there is little risk of flooding.

The land surface

Some natural flood protection occurs when water can drain away into the soil. Trees help the water drain into the ground by breaking up the earth with their roots. When trees are removed from an area and not replanted, as in parts of the Himalayas, water is not soaked up so well by the soil. Rain runs quickly off the surface, often washing away the soil with it. Replanting trees is one way of helping to prevent floods.

Planning ahead and being prepared help to prevent floods. The use of technology such as the building of dams, barriers, or dikes can help to prevent disaster in areas that are prone to flooding.

Ways to prevent floods or lessen flood damage

Dikes or levees	Building up banks
Floodwalls	Floodproofing houses
Channels	Building on high ground
Reservoirs	Increasing emergency services
River diversion	Moving people to safer places
Reforestation	Providing flood warnings
Terracing	Changing farming methods

Above: Dams, like this one in Austria, can control the flow of water in rivers, helping to prevent floods. Sometimes, though, dams can burst and cause terrifying floods.

Left: The gates of the Thames Barrier can be raised or lowered. When a storm surge threatens London the gates can be lowered to stop flood water from flowing upstream.

Dams

Building a dam creates a reservoir, which may take up extra water when there is heavy rain. This stops storm water from rushing downstream and flooding the valley below. During the year the stored water can be let out in a steady stream and put to good use.

In China a huge dam was built on the Yellow River to help control flooding. However, the river brings so much silt downstream with it that the dam has become choked. Other dams in the world have this problem, too.

Barriers

London is in great danger from flooding because it is so low-lying. If a storm surge much bigger than the one in 1953 came in from the North Sea, a huge area could be flooded. To prevent a storm surge from reaching the heart of London, the Thames Barrier was built. It has ten steel gates that can be raised to block the river when a flood threatens.

Dikes and levees

The Netherlands' rich but low-lying farmland has been protected by dikes for hundreds of years. The dikes have been raised and strengthened since the 1953 disaster. In the United States, the Mississippi is surrounded by hundreds of levees to control flooding. The levees are so wide that they have roads running along the top, and the whole system of levees is longer than the Great Wall of China.

THE BENEFITS OF FLOODS

Some of the most fertile farming land in the world lies beside great rivers. When the rivers overflow, the floods leave behind sediment rich with nutrients. In the past, most towns and cities were built on flood plains. This was because people thought that the benefits of living on fertile land outweighed the disadvantages of occasional flooding.

Paddy fields in south China filled with water diverted from a local river.

The Nile Delta

Farmers of the Nile delta used to rely on the regular floods for good crops. People knew that the flooding would happen, so they were prepared for it. After the floodwater had died down they planted their crops. In this way farming in the Nile Delta was able to feed the people of Egypt for thousands of years. In more recent times people wanted the river controlled so they could grow crops all year round, so the Aswan High Dam was built across the Nile. Because of the dam the river no longer floods, and farmers in the Nile Delta now have to flood their fields artificially and use chemical fertilizers.

Making floods

Many farmers grow their crops on floodplains next to rivers. In Asia, farmers rely on rivers to bring fresh water to their paddy fields. Water is diverted from rivers to flood these lands. As in the Nile Delta, the artificially flooded fields are a great benefit to farmers.

The Aswan High Dam in Egypt. It controls the water of the Nile River.

1. House on stilts

From Asia to the Amazon, many of the people who live near rivers in developing countries build their houses on stilts and use boats for travel when the river floods. The stilts stand in the ground and keep the houses well above the water level. When there is heavy rain and the river floods, the houses usually stay safe and dry.

Materials:
Cardboard
Glue
4 wooden sticks about
    8 inches long
4 pebbles
Modeling clay
Scissors

Method:

1. Cut out a rectangular cardboard base for the house. Push the sticks halfway through the base near each of the corners.

2. Cut out four cardboard rectangles for the walls of the house, and make holes for the windows and doors. Glue the walls to the base and to the sticks. Cut and glue two rectangles of cardboard to make a sloping roof.

3. Attach a small pebble to the bottom of each stick with modeling clay. Stand you model in a pan of water.

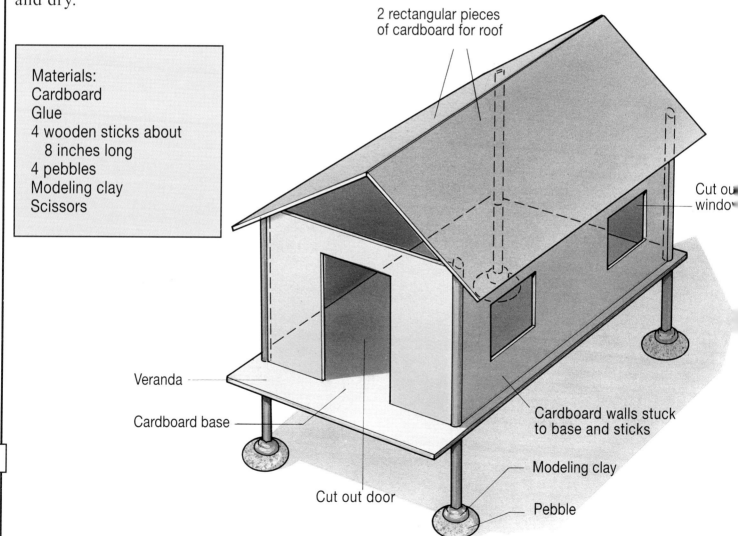

2 rectangular pieces
of cardboard for roof

Cut ou
windo

Veranda

Cardboard base

Cut out door

Cardboard walls stuck
to base and sticks

Modeling clay

Pebble

2. Making a rain gauge

A rain gauge is an instrument used to measure rainfall. It is quite easy to make your own rain gauge to see how much water falls where you live. A lot of rain produces only a little water in a jam jar, so to make it easier, you should catch the water in one jar and put it in a taller, thinner jar or glass to measure it. Remember that your readings will be more accurate if you position your jam jar away from trees and buildings to collect rain.

Method:

1. Draw a scale in inches on a piece of paper. Using the tape, attach this scale to the jar as in the picture. Fill the jar with water up to 1 inch.

2. Stick a plain strip of paper to the side of the thin jar or glass. Pour the water from the jam jar into it. Mark on the paper where the water level comes. Label it "1 in."

3. Repeat with 2 inches of water in the jam jar, and mark the 2-inches level on the thin glass. Do the same with 3 inches and up until near the top of the thin glass. Divide the marks on the thin glass into fractions of an inch.

4. Put the jam jar outside on the grass. Every rainy day collect the rainwater, pour it into the thin glass, and record the amount of rain that has fallen.

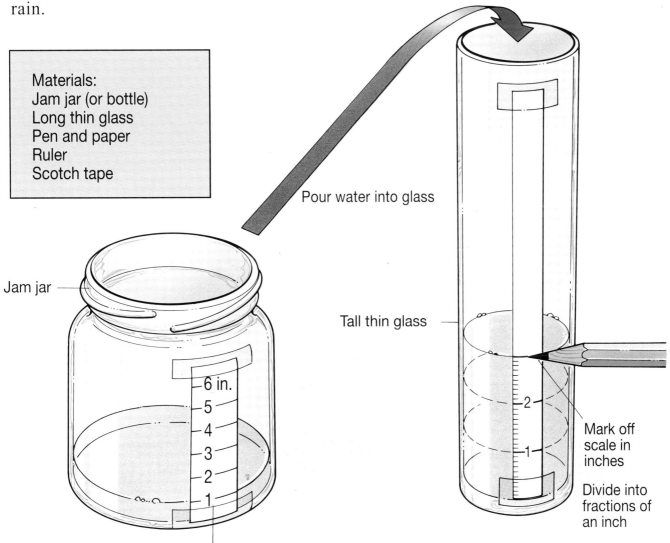

Materials:
Jam jar (or bottle)
Long thin glass
Pen and paper
Ruler
Scotch tape

Pour water into glass

Jam jar

Tall thin glass

6 in.
5
4
3
2
1

2

1

Mark off scale in inches

Divide into fractions of an inch

Mark scale in inches

29

GLOSSARY

CYCLONE A tropical storm or hurricane.

DEBRIS The pieces of something that has been destroyed or broken.

DEFORESTATION The removal of the trees in an area.

DELTA A flat, fan-shaped area where a river splits into many channels at the end of its course.

DEVELOPING COUNTRIES The poor countries of the world, in which there is very little industry and people depend mainly on farming.

DIKE An earth bank built to keep out the sea and prevent an area of land from flooding.

DYSENTERY An infectious disease caused by eating food or drinking water containing certain germs.

FERTILIZER Something added to soil to make it richer and so help plants grow.

FLOODPLAIN The flat land beside rivers where they flood and drop sediment.

LEGENDS Stories from long ago that have been passed on from one generation to the next.

LEVEES Earth banks along the side of a river.

MONSOON A rainy season when winds blow from the sea and bring heavy rain.

NUTRIENTS Mineral substances in the earth that are necessary for the growth of plants.

PADDY FIELDS Flooded fields in which rice is grown.

POLLUTED Unclean or poisoned with waste, rubbish, or dirt.

RESERVOIR A lake or large tank in which water is collected and stored.

SEDIMENT Materials such as clay, sand, gravel, or stones carried by a river.

SILT Very fine material carried by a river.

STARVATION Death resulting from lack of food.

SUBMERGED Completely covered by water.

VICTIM A person who suffers, usually because of events beyond their control.

BOOKS TO READ

Dixon, Dougal. *The Changing Earth*.
Young Geographer. Thomson Learning, 1993.

Knapp, Brian. *Flood*. World Disasters.
Austin, TX: Steck-Vaughn, 1990.

Micallef, Mary. *Floods and Droughts*.
Carthage, IL: Good Apple, 1985.

Richardson, Joy. *The Water Cycle*. Picture
Science. New York: Franklin Watts, 1992.

Walker, Jane. *Tidal Waves and Flooding*.
Natural Disasters. New York: Franklin Watts,
1992.

Waters, John. *Flood!* Nature's Disasters.
New York: Crestwood House, 1991.

Wood, Tim. *Natural Disasters*. The World's
Disasters. New York: Thomson Learning, 1993.

Picture acknowledgments

The publishers would like to thank the following for
allowing their photographs to be reproduced in this book:
Camera Press 14 (top); Forestry Commission 23
(bottom); the Hutchison Library *cover*, 6/7 (Lyn Gambles);
Panos Pictures 17 (Penny Tweedie), 21, 23 (top); Photri
9; Rex Features 2/3 (Roger Hutchings), 4, 10, 10/11, 16,
20; Topham Picture Library 12, 15, 19, 27; Julia Waterlow
22, 24, 26/27 (both); Zefa Picture Library 25.

INDEX